the Ring

an original Irish tale
by
Teresa Bateman

Illustrated by
Omar Rayyan

holiday house/new york

To my mother and father who taught me the importance of truth,
and the entertainment value of blarney.
TB

To my Irish in-laws, who should note:
All persons depicted in this book are fictitious.
Any resemblance to actual persons is purely coincidental.
OR

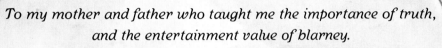
Text copyright © 1997 by Teresa Bateman
Illustrations copyright © 1997 by Omar Rayyan
All rights reserved
Printed in the United States of America

Library of Congress Cataloging-in-Publication Data
Bateman, Teresa.
The Ring of Truth / Teresa Bateman; illustrated by Omar Rayyan. —
1st ed.
p.   cm.
Summary: After the king of the leprechauns bestows on him the Ring
of Truth, Patrick O'Kelley no longer expects to win a blarney
contest.
ISBN 0-8234-1255-5 (hardcover: alk. paper)
[1. Fairy tales.] I. Rayyan, Omar, ill. II. Title.
PZ8.B3015Ri   1997   96-5336   CIP   AC
[E]—dc20

ISBN 0-8234-1518-X (pbk.)

atrick O'Kelley was a peddler of scarves and trinkets, with a habit of telling magnificent lies. He traveled from village to village, a pack on his back and a wild story on his lips, never telling the truth when a lie would do. Indeed, folks said he must have kissed the Blarney Stone and caught a bit of it in his teeth, for the legend had it that all those who kissed the stone in Blarney Castle, near Cork, would be skilled in flattery.

Patrick was proud and cocky about his stories, but his loose tongue proved his undoing.

One day he heard there was going to be a blarney contest in the county of Donegal. The prize was a pot of gold. Naturally Patrick thought he was the most likely to win the contest.

"Why," said he, "I can spout better blarney than the king of the leprechauns himself."

As you might expect, word of Patrick's prideful boast made its way under the mountain to the home of the leprechaun king. Leprechauns consider blarney an art form, and themselves its best artists. When the king heard of Patrick's bold statement, his eyes flashed green lightning.

"That Patrick O'Kelley," the king told his followers. "He's fair puffed up with blarney, thinking he's as good as any one of us. It's time he was taught a lesson."

That night Patrick O'Kelley lay down to sleep under an oak tree, but, when he awoke, he was someplace else.

He was in a huge room with a ceiling that stretched out
of sight, and walls that were lined with gold and silver.
Trees grew there, with leaves of diamond and amethyst.

He heard a clinking sound and sat up. He looked
around and saw that the ground was covered with gold
coins.

Patrick rubbed his eyes, thinking he was still asleep, but when he opened them again, they caught the sparkle of silver coins among the gold, and jewels as well. He started to slip some of the riches into his pockets when a trumpet sounded.

Looking up, he saw the king of the leprechauns on a golden throne, being carried in by four tiny ponies no larger than dogs.

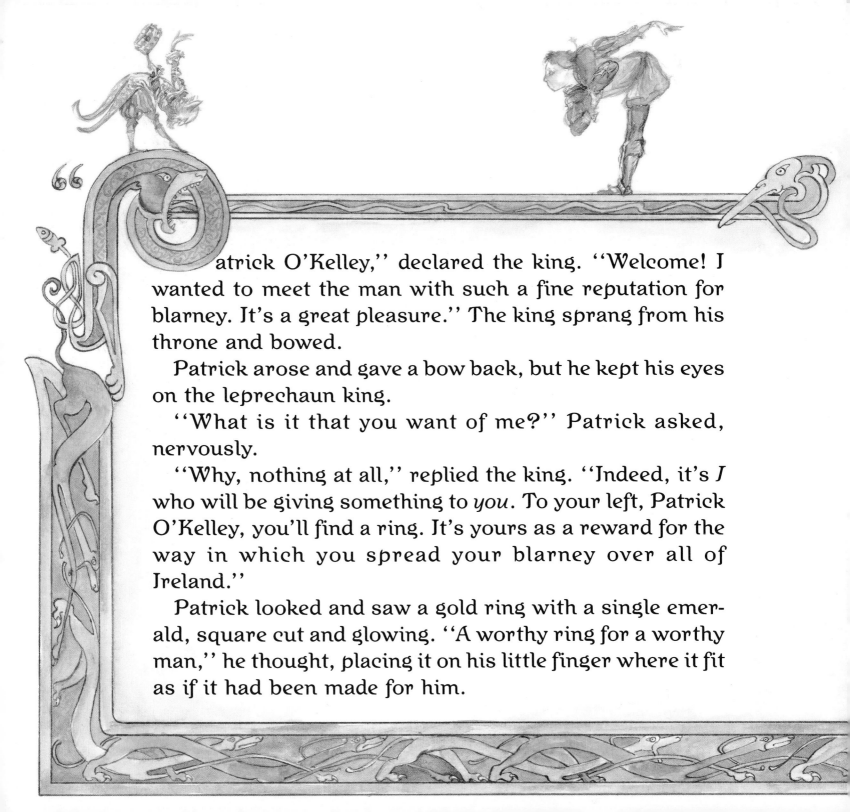

"atrick O'Kelley," declared the king. "Welcome! I wanted to meet the man with such a fine reputation for blarney. It's a great pleasure." The king sprang from his throne and bowed.

Patrick arose and gave a bow back, but he kept his eyes on the leprechaun king.

"What is it that you want of me?" Patrick asked, nervously.

"Why, nothing at all," replied the king. "Indeed, it's *I* who will be giving something to *you*. To your left, Patrick O'Kelley, you'll find a ring. It's yours as a reward for the way in which you spread your blarney over all of Ireland."

Patrick looked and saw a gold ring with a single emerald, square cut and glowing. "A worthy ring for a worthy man," he thought, placing it on his little finger where it fit as if it had been made for him.

"What have I done to earn such a reward?" Patrick asked.

"Do you think you're the only one who can talk blarney?" laughed the leprechaun. "That's no reward, but a punishment for your pride. You'll never take that ring off again, for it's the Ring of Truth. The man who wears it can tell nothing but the plain truth for the rest of his days. Now let's see how well you get on in life without your pack of lies!"

There was a flash of light, and when Patrick O'Kelley opened his eyes, he was lying beneath the oak tree again.

"So, 'twas a dream after all," he mumbled, and turned over for a bit more sleep. But something hard was pressing against his cheek. He looked down, and there on his hand was the gold ring with the square emerald.

Patrick sat up. He started to say, "It didn't happen. It isn't real." But what came out was, "It *did* happen. It *is* real." The absolute truth, and only that.

He tried to pull off the ring, but he might as well have tried to remove his own finger. It was stuck there, just as the king of the leprechauns had said. Neither soap nor struggle could remove it, and Patrick had the sinking feeling that his life was going to change, and not for the better.

Indeed he was right, because from then on everywhere he went, peddling his goods, he told only the truth. No longer could he lie to the ladies about how beautiful they looked in his kerchiefs and baubles. If they looked ridiculous, well, he had to tell them so. This was not good for business.

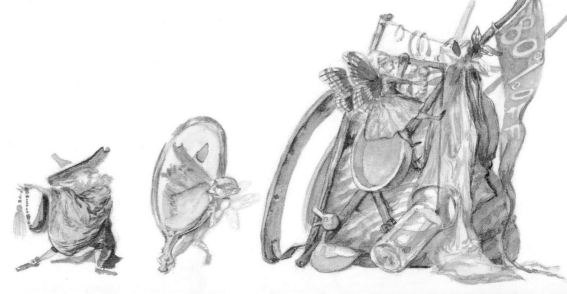

Worse, people who had suffered his peddling for the chance to hear his blarney were now sore disappointed, and he was run out of first one village, then another.

So it was that he found himself on the road to Donegal, where his reputation was still sound. He knew the blarney contest was completely out of the question, but thought of the crowds who would attend. Surely he could get some of them to buy his wares, if only he could keep his tongue still.

When Patrick entered the town the streets were silent, for all had gathered at the main hall to hear the liars' contest. Curious, he decided to sneak into the back of the room, and hear the competition he would have faced before his encounter with the leprechaun king.

But the first person who saw him, not having heard of his recent misfortune, sent up a cry.

"Here's Patrick O'Kelley! He's sure to win!"

Before he could say a word, he was being hustled to the stage, and soon found himself in line for the contest, unable to slip away.

As the day wore on the stories grew wilder and more fantastic—potatoes as big as mountains, changelings, magic harps, and enchanted castles.

Poor Patrick O'Kelley. When the time came for him to speak, he knew he would be disgraced. He stepped forward and, having no choice, told the plain truth.

"I'm sorry," said he. "I cannot enter this contest. You see, I grew so good at blarney that the king of the leprechauns himself was angry with me and took me to his kingdom beneath the earth, where gold and silver walls rise up forever and the trees bear diamonds and amethysts. Why, the very ground itself is covered with riches—gold and silver coins and sparkling jewels."

There was a hushed silence.

"There the king of the leprechauns himself came to me, carried on a gold throne by four tiny horses, no taller than my knee. He got down and he bowed to *me*, Patrick O'Kelley. Indeed. I should have been suspicious even then. He told me he was going to reward me for the fine quality of my blarney."

A snort of disbelief interrupted him.

"Aye, I can see you doubt my word. How I wish I'd doubted his, for he gave me a fine gold ring with an emerald. Only after I placed it on my finger did he tell me of the ring's curse. 'It's the Ring of Truth!' he said. 'The man who wears that ring can tell nothing but the plain truth for the rest of his days.'"

"And so it's been since that day," Patrick O'Kelley continued sadly. "I cannot compete in this blarney contest, for here on my finger is the Ring of Truth, and I cannot get it off, no matter how I try!"

There was a long silence, then the room burst into laughter.

"That's the biggest pack of blarney I've ever heard," declared the judge.

So Patrick O'Kelley won the pot of gold. He protested, ever truthful, that it wasn't blarney at all, but nobody believed him. So what could he do but accept his good fortune?

He had learned a lesson, however. With half the gold, he bought a plot of land and a wee cottage and settled down free of want for the rest of his days. The other half he laid at the foot of the oak tree, as an apology to the leprechaun king.

erhaps the king accepted his apology, for Patrick was often invited back to visit the leprechauns. He wore the emerald ring all his life, but never lacked for tales of the fair folk. Or perhaps the leprechaun king was still playing a joke. For, though Patrick often told tales of the time he spent in that magical kingdom beneath the ground, nobody ever believed him.